Captain Dargo: Born to Serve

DARGO

Capitán Dargo: Nacido para Servir

By M. J. McCluskey

Be strong and brave like DARGO!
M. J. McCluskey

Balboa Press books may be ordered through booksellers or by contacting:

Balboa Press
A Division of Hay House
1663 Liberty Drive
Bloomington, IN 47403
www.balboapress.com
1 (877) 407-4847

Because of the dynamic nature of the Internet, any web addresses or links contained in this book may have changed since publication and may no longer be valid. The views expressed in this work are solely those of the author and do not necessarily reflect the views of the publisher, and the publisher hereby disclaims any responsibility for them.

Any people depicted in stock imagery provided by Getty Images are models, and such images are being used for illustrative purposes only.
Certain stock imagery © Getty Images.

ISBN: 978-1-9822-4420-0 (sc)
ISBN: 978-1-9822-4422-4 (hc)
ISBN: 978-1-9822-4421-7 (e)

Library of Congress Control Number: 2020904615

Printed in the United States of America.

Balboa Press rev. date: 03/11/2020

BALBOA.PRESS

This book is dedicated to K9 Captain Dargo and his partner Lt. David Godfrey of the York County, PA Sheriff's Office.

Thank you for welcoming me into your lives for the last two years! I have nothing but admiration for all that you and all K9 officers and partners do 24/7/365.

"There he is! I see him!"

Asher turned and stood up as tall as he could to get a better look at Captain Dargo and Lt. Dave as they walked into the room.

Dargo knew this was a special day. He walked proudly with his head held high. Today he was getting an award from the Sheriff for bravery.

"¡Ahí está!" "¡Lo veo!"

Asher volteó y se levantó tan alto como pudo para ver mejor al capitán Dargo y el teniente David mientras entraban a la habitación.

Dargo sabía que éste era un día especial. Caminaba orgullosamente con su cabeza en alto. Hoy estaba recibiendo un premio del sheriff por valentía.

Dargo thought back to when he was a puppy…

I was born on November 13, 2011 in Czechoslovakia, a country far away in Europe. I was named Dargo Bett Silver and I was born to be a K9 police dog. This is my story.

I played with all of the other puppies, but I dreamed of the day I could go to work as a K9 police officer.

Dargo comenzó a recordar cuando era un cachorro…

Nací el 13 de noviembre de 2011 en Checoslovaquia, un país muy lejos en Europa. Fui nombrado Dargo Bett Silver y nací para ser un perro policía. Ésta es mi historia.

Jugaba con todos los demás cachorros, pero soñaba con el día que pudiera ir a trabajar como perro policía.

One day, a man from America came to visit. I was only one year old. This man was going to take some special German Shepherd puppies back to America to train at his police dog school.

I was so happy when he picked me to be one of the special puppies.

I was excited to start living the K9 life!

Un día, un hombre de los Estados Unidos vino a visitar. Yo sólo tenía un año. Este hombre quería llevar a algunos cachorros pastores alemanes especiales a los Estados Unidos para entrenarles en su escuela de perros policía.

Yo estaba tan contento cuando me escogió para ser uno de los cachorros especiales.

¡Estaba emocionado de empezar a vivir la vida de perro policía!

In America, there were some special musicians in York, PA who wanted to help the County Sheriff's Office get another K9. They donated money to buy a police dog.

En los Estados Unidos, habían unos músicos especiales en York, Pensilvania, que querían ayudar a la oficina del sheriff del condado a conseguir otro perro policía. Donaron dinero para comprarlo.

Lt. Dave traveled to the police dog school in Ohio to select his new K9 partner. He looked at many dogs.

When he saw me, he knew that we would be good partners. I thought so too. I was so glad that Lt. Dave picked me.

El teniente David viajó a la escuela de perros policía en Ohio para elegir a su nueva pareja canina.

Cuando me vió, él sabía que íbamos a ser buenos compañeros. Yo pensé lo mismo. Yo estaba tan contento que el teniente David me había escogido.

Now our work really started. We had to go to school together. Every day for 6 weeks, Lt. Dave and I went to class. We both had to study and we had to learn to work together as a team.

I am an explosives dog. That means I can find bombs and guns and other things that can hurt people. I needed to learn many different smells so that I could find the explosives. I worked hard, and so did Lt. Dave.

Ahora nuestro trabajo realmente había comenzado. Teníamos que ir a la escuela juntos. Todos los días por 6 semanas, el teniente David y yo íbamos a la clase. Ambos teníamos que estudiar y teníamos que trabajar juntos como equipo.

Yo soy un perro detector de explosivos. Eso quiere decir que puedo encontrar bombas y armas y otras cosas que pueden lastimar a las personas. Necesitaba conocer muchos olores diferentes para que pudiera encontrar los explosivos. Trabajaba duro, y el teniente David también.

Did you know that Lt. Dave talks to me in a special language when we are working? He gives me commands in German! That's how I know that it is time to go to work.

At the end of the school, I had to take a test. I had to get every answer right in identifying the smells.

¿Sabías que el teniente David me habla en un idioma especial cuando estamos trabajando? ¡Me habla en alemán! Así es cómo sé que es hora para ir a trabajar.

Al final de la escuela, Tuve que hacer un examen. Tuve que contestar todas las preguntas correctamente en identificar los olores.

I got 100% on my test and passed with flying colors! We were ready for graduation.

At graduation, I became Captain Dargo of the York County Sheriff's Office. I outrank Lt. Dave because Lt. Dave has to trust and follow me when we are working.

¡Saqué 100% en mi examen y lo hice como pan comido! Estábamos listos para la graduación.

En la graduación, volví capitán Dargo de la oficina del sheriff del condado de York. Le superé al teniente David porque el teniente David tiene que confiar y seguirme cuando estamos trabajando.

We were ready to go home to York and settle into our new life together.

I go to work in the Courthouse every day with Lt. Dave.

Lt. Lou, another K9 officer, was already in the Sheriff's Office, and he helped to teach me too.

I have my own special workplace in the Sheriff's Office. Sometimes Lt. Dave lets me sit with him at his desk. It was a whole lot easier to do when I was little!

Estábamos listos para regresar a casa en York y asentarnos en nuestra nueva vida juntos.

Voy al trabajo en la corte todos los días con el teniente David.

El teniente Lou, otro oficial de la policía canina, ya estaba listo en la oficina del sheriff, y él también ayudó a enseñarme.

Tengo mi propio lugar especial de trabajo en la oficina del sheriff. A veces el teniente David me deja sentarme con él en su escritorio. ¡Era mucho más fácil cuando era pequeño!

My most important job is to find explosives, but I can do a lot of other jobs too.

For every different type of job, I wear a different collar. This helps me know what job I am doing.

I can find missing children or people who are lost.

Mi trabajo más importante es encontrar explosivos, pero puedo hacer otros trabajos también.

Para cada tipo de trabajo, uso un collar diferente. Éste me ayuda a saber qué trabajo estoy haciendo.

Puedo encontrar a niños o personas que están perdidos.

I can find people who are hiding from the police, even if they are hiding in a ceiling.

I get very excited when I am working. Sometimes my bark is very, very loud. I REALLY like to bark!

Puedo encontrar a personas que se están escondiendo de la policía, incluso si se esconden en un techo.

Me emociono mucho cuando estoy trabajando. A veces mi ladrido es muy, muy alto. ¡A mí REALMENTE me gusta ladrar!

I can find things that a person throws away when they are running from the police.

I can do that because I capture smells on my tongue.

Puedo encontrar cosas que una persona tira cuando huye de la policía.

Lo puedo hacer porque capturo olores con mi lengua.

When I am working, I think I am chasing a bunny rabbit. This is so much fun.

When I find what I am looking for, I sit still and stare at it until Lt. Dave and the other officers come.

I get rewarded and get to play with my bunny! Lt. Dave says that it's just a piece of fire hose that is taped, but I know better. It's a bunny!

Cuando estoy trabajando, imagino que estoy siguiendo un conejito. Esto es muy divertido.

Cuando encuentro lo que estoy buscando, me siento ahí y lo miro hasta que el teniente David y los demás policías vengan.

¡Me recompensan y puedo jugar con mi conejito! El teniente David dice que sólo es un trozo de manguera contra incendios que está pegado, pero yo sé mejor. ¡Es un conejito!

One part of my job that I really like is meeting new boys and girls, and grown-ups too. I show them what I can do when I am working. I make lots of friends everywhere I go.

I get to teach boys and girls that police officers and sheriff deputies are their friends. I like it a lot when the boys and girls pet and hug me.

Una parte de mi trabajo que realmente me gusta es conocer a nuevos niños y niñas, y adultos también. Les enseño lo que puedo hacer cuando estoy trabajando. Hago muchos amigos en todas partes.

Puedo enseñar a niños y niñas que los policías y los sheriffs son sus amigos. Me gusta mucho cuando los niños me acarician y me abrazan.

Every year, I go to work at the York Fair. Just like boys and girls, I have my favorite places to eat.

Some days, I go to a baseball game and watch the York Revolution. I am friends with Downtown!

Todos los años, voy a trabajar en la feria de York. Como los niños y niñas, tengo mis lugares favoritos para comer.

Algunos días, voy a un partido de beisbol y miro el equipo de York Revolution. ¡Soy amigo de Downtown!

I even have a special police cruiser that is just for me to ride in.

Lt. Dave gets to drive - most of the time!

Incluso tengo un carro policía especial que es solamente para que yo vaya.

El teniente David maneja - ¡la mayoría del tiempo!

Other days, I go to a school or a library to teach children what I do as a K9 officer.

I even go to spaghetti dinners to help raise money to take care of the dogs in the Sheriff's Office.

Otros días, voy a una escuela o una biblioteca para enseñarles a los niños qué hago como perro policía.

Incluso voy a cenas de espagueti para recaudar fondos para el cuidado de los perros de la oficina del sheriff.

I love my job, and I am very good at it.

Did you know that I am one of four dogs in the Sheriff's Office? We all have important jobs to keep boys and girls safe.

Me encanta mi trabajo, y soy muy bueno en ello.

¿Sabías que soy uno de cuatro perros en la oficina del sheriff? Todos de nosotros tenemos trabajos importantes para mantener seguros a los niños y niñas.

At the end of the work day, I go home with Lt. Dave. I live with him and his family. I get to play with the other dogs in the house. The little Chihuahua likes to boss me around!

Al final del día de trabajo, regreso a casa con el teniente David. Vivo con él y su familia. Puedo jugar con los otros perros en la casa. ¡A la chihuahua pequeña le gusta decirme qué hacer!

I love my K9 officer life.

Me encanta mi vida de perro policía.

Coming home from police dog school

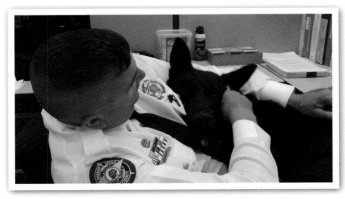

Dargo helps Lt. Dave

A well-deserved break

Asher walking Dargo

Captain Dargo and Lt. Lou

Captain Dargo and service dog Philly

Photo Credit - Kerri Bennett

Storytelling and writing have always been a part of M. J. McCluskey's life. A career in finance, technology, and even teaching, finally opened a way for her to become a children's book author when a corporate reorganization included the elimination of her position.

M. J. has a passion for literacy, imagination, and exploring the world through books. She wants to share these passions with every child.

She lives in York, PA and is the mother of two adult children.